CAMILA
THE TALENT SHOW STAR

written by ALICIA SALAZAR

illustrated by THAIS DAMIÃO

PICTURE WINDOW BOOKS
a capstone imprint

Published by Picture Window Books, an imprint of Capstone
1710 Roe Crest Drive, North Mankato, Minnesota 56003
capstonepub.com

Library of Congress Cataloging-in-Publication Data
Names: Salazar, Alicia, 1973- author. | Damião, Thais, illustrator. |
Salazar, Alicia, 1973- Camila the star.
Title: Camila the talent show star / by Alicia Salazar ; illustrated by
Thais Damião.
Description: North Mankato, Minnesota : Picture Window Books, an imprint
of Capstone, [2022] | Series: Camila the star | Audience: Ages 5-7. | Audience:
Grades K-1. | Summary: Every year Camila's school has a talent show, and
Camila wants to sing her favorite song, but Ruby, a new girl, has already signed
up to sing the same song. Camila is so mad she decides not to compete at all—
until Ruby suggests that they sing together. Camila discovers sometimes two
voices are better than one. Includes suggestions for creating your own talent
show.
Identifiers: LCCN 2021033320 (print) | LCCN 2021033321 (ebook) | ISBN
9781663958716 (hardcover) | ISBN 9781666331547 (paperback) | ISBN
9781666331554 (pdf)
Subjects: LCSH: Hispanic American girls—Juvenile fiction. | Talent shows—
Juvenile fiction. | Singing—Juvenile fiction. | Anger—Juvenile fiction. |
Friendship—Juvenile fiction. | CYAC: Talent shows—Fiction. | Singing—
Fiction. | Friendship—Fiction. | Hispanic Americans—Fiction.
Classification: LCC PZ7.1.S2483 Cc 2022 (print) | LCC PZ7.1.S2483 (ebook) |
DDC [E]—dc23
LC record available at https://lccn.loc.gov/2021033320
LC ebook record available at https://lccn.loc.gov/2021033321

Designer: Hilary Wacholz

Printed and bound in the USA. PO4608

TABLE OF CONTENTS

Meet Camila and Her Family

Papá

Mamá

Ana, age 14

Andres, age 10

Camila, age 7

Spanish Glossary

canción (cahn-SEE-OHN)—song

no es justo (noh ehs HOO-stoh)—it's not fair

piénsalo (PEE-EHN-sa-loh)—think about it

primer plano (pree-MEHR PLAH-noh)—spotlight

Chapter 1

THE SAME SONG

On a Monday morning in April, Mrs. Jolly shared some news. The end-of-year talent show would be in a few weeks.

Camila had been waiting for the show all year.

"I'll be a star!" she said.

"Think about what you want to do for the show. Then fill out the sign-up sheet," said Mrs. Jolly.

Camila knew exactly what she wanted to do.

She wanted to sing her favorite **canción**, "Love Is a Jewel."

As soon as she finished her work, Camila went to sign up. Ruby, the new girl, had already signed up.

And she was singing the same **canción** Camila wanted to sing!

TALENT SHOW

SIGN UP HERE

1. Ruby – Love Is a Jewel

Camila showed her teacher the sheet. "But Mrs. Jolly," she said, "I wanted to sing 'Love Is a Jewel.'"

"Sorry," said her teacher. "Ruby signed up first. You can sing a different song."

Camila slammed her pencil
down on her desk.

"**No es justo**," she thought.

Camila tried to think of another song to sing.

"Silly Games?"

"Flower Girls?"

"Sharks?"

But those weren't her favorite songs.

"I just won't be in the talent show this year," she thought.

Chapter 2

SPITTING MAD

Camila frowned for the rest of the day.

She didn't finish her work.

She stomped to the car when Mamá picked her up.

Mamá asked what was wrong.

"I'm not going to be in the talent show," Camila spit out.

"But you have been talking about the talent show all year," said Mamá.

"Exactly," said Camila. "Ruby ruined my plans."

"You have a week before sign-ups are closed," said Mamá. "**Piénsalo**."

Camila thought about it.

Every time she thought about it, she narrowed her eyes and clenched her fists.

At school, she avoided Ruby. She didn't sit with her at lunch. She didn't talk to her in small group.

In music class on Thursday, everyone was practicing for the talent show.

Only Camila was standing alone with her arms crossed and her eyes squinted.

She watched Ruby sing.

"She should wear a special outfit," Camila thought.

Ruby hit a high note.

"She should have a shiny background," Camila thought.

Ruby danced a few steps.

"She should . . ."

Camila couldn't take it anymore. She forgot how mad she was at Ruby.

Chapter 3

SHARING THE SPOTLIGHT

"Um, Ruby," Camila said. She tapped Ruby on the shoulder. "I was just watching you. Do you want to hear some ideas about your act?"

"You're Camila, right?" Ruby asked. "The other kids say you are a great singer."

Camila beamed. "Thanks," she said. "'Love Is a Jewel' is my favorite song."

"You should be singing it in the talent show!" said Ruby.

Camila's face went red. How could she tell her?

"But you signed up before me," said Camila.

"What if we sing it together?" said Ruby.

"You mean be stars together?" Camila asked.

"It's okay with me," said Ruby. "What about you?"

"Why is Ruby being so nice to me?" Camila thought. She could feel her anger fading.

Camila looked at the stage.
If she performed with Ruby,
she would have to share the
primer plano.

If she didn't perform at all,
there wouldn't be a **primer
plano** for her.

She loved the song "Love Is a Jewel." She had planned all year to sing it in the show.

"Okay," Camila said. "Let's do it."

The girls gave each other a high five.

The night of the talent show came. The chairs were filled with moms and dads, brothers and sisters.

Camila and Ruby watched
the other students.
One boy juggled.

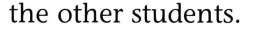

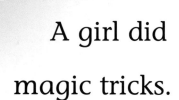

A girl did

magic tricks.

A set of

twins tap

danced.

When it was their turn, the new friends gave each other a fist bump. Then they walked onstage.

"Thanks for being a star with me," Ruby said.

"Thanks for letting me share your spotlight," said Camila.

Host a Talent Show!

Do you have a secret (or not-so-secret) talent? What about your friends and family? Put on a neighborhood talent show and let those talents shine!

WHAT YOU DO

1. Chose a time and place for the talent show. Good places are your backyard or a park. Give performers at least one week to prepare. Talk to a grown-up to make sure your time and place work.

2. Invite people to perform in the talent show. Some people might think they don't have any talents, but that's not true. Help your friends think of ideas. Here are a few to get started:

   - Play an instrument, like the recorder or drums. Even a snappy kazoo song is fun!

   - Be a comedian and tell some jokes.

   - Do a live painting. Play some music and paint in rhythm to the music.

   - Show off your ball skills! Soccer juggling or basketball tricks are fun to watch.

3. Plan your stage and audience areas. You can ask your audience to bring blankets or chairs to sit on if you don't have enough seats.

4. Make a poster to get the word out about your talent show. If you are asking people to bring their own seats, be sure to include that on the poster. Deliver copies to your friends and family members. Hang a few around the neighborhood.

5. Make and share a schedule for the order of performances. You might want to make a program of the schedule and hand out copies at the show.

6. It's showtime! Enjoy the talents of your friends and family, and maybe share a talent of your own.

Glossary

avoid (uh-VOYD)—to stay away from someone or something

clench (KLENCH)—a close tightly

jewel (JOO-uhl)—a valuable stone that is often cut and polished to sparkle

onstage (ON-stayj)—on the part of a stage that can be seen by people in the audience

spotlight (SPOT-lyte)—a spot of light used to light up a particular area or person during performances; the audience pays the most attention to those in the spotlight

squint (SKWINT)—to look with eyes partly closed

talent show (TAL-uhnt SHOH)—a special event where performers share acts

Think About the Story

1. How did Camila feel when she realized Ruby had signed up to sing "Love Is a Jewel"? List three examples from the story that give clues as to how she felt.

2. Imagine that Camila went through with her decision to skip performing in the talent show. How do you think she would have felt watching her classmates perform, knowing she would not get to? Why?

3. Imagine you were performing in a talent show. What would your act be? Write a paragraph about it.

4. Create a poster for Camila's school talent show. Be sure to include details like when, where, and who. You can get some of these details from the story, and you can make up the other details.

About the Author

Alicia Salazar is a Mexican American children's book author who has written for blogs, magazines, and educational publishers. She was also once an elementary school teacher and a marine biologist. She currently lives in the suburbs of Houston, Texas, but is a city girl at heart. When Alicia is not dreaming up new adventures to experience, she is turning her adventures into stories for kids.

About the Illustrator

Thais Damião is a Brazilian illustrator and graphic designer. Born and raised in a small city in Rio de Janeiro State, Brazil, she spent her childhood playing with her brother and cousins and drawing all the time. Her illustrations are dedicated to children and inspired by nature and friendship. Thais currently lives in California.